The Hyena Laughs at Night

by
Anne Schraff

Perfection Learning® Corporation
Logan, Iowa 51546

Cover Illustration: Doug Knutson
Cover Design: Deborah Lea Bell

For Information, contact:
Perfection Learning® Corporation
1000 North Second Avenue, P.O. Box 500
Logan, Iowa 51546-1099.
Tel: 1-800-831-4190 • Fax: 1-712-644-2392

Paperback ISBN 0-7891-4925-7
Cover Craft® ISBN 0-7807-8006-x
Printed in the U.S.A.

5 6 7 8 9 10 PP 08 07 06 05 04 03

1   Dustin Brand's hand moved swiftly over his paper as he snatched quick glances at his geometry teacher. He smiled to himself, watching the exaggerated image of Mrs. Blount emerging under the strokes of his pencil. Her plump cheeks had always reminded Dustin of a chipmunk's cheeks swollen with nuts. He captured her dark, piercing eyes that gave her the stern look of an owl. Then he duplicated a little bow mouth wedged between her cheeks. He was just starting on her curly blond hair when Mrs. Blount's shrill voice rang through the classroom.

"Dustin! Pass that paper to the front, please. I want to be sure you're getting this." The teacher had a look of sinister glee on her face as if she were well aware that Dustin's paper did not contain geometry problems.

Dustin knew Mrs. Blount was expecting to find a personal message or a dirty joke. She seemed to enjoy reading such things aloud, censoring the most vulgar words but leaving no doubt as to their meanings. Dustin remembered that the week before she'd had a great time with Emma McCall's passionate note to her boyfriend. Now Mrs. Blount waited with obvious relish as Dustin's paper was passed to the front. Each student who handled it began to laugh, some more loudly than others. Dustin saw Mrs. Blount frown as her curiosity was aroused.

Finally, the paper made its way into the teacher's hands. Muffled giggles and whispers filled the room as the students in Dustin's row spread the word about the picture.

Mrs. Blount recognized herself at once. Her eyes widened, and her mouth dropped in dismay. "Well, Mr. Brand," she said. "I see that drawing cartoons of your teacher is more important to you than geometry."

Dustin noticed that he had become "Mr. Brand," a sure sign that Mrs. Blount was angry at him.

"Um, Mrs. Blount," Dustin began. He wanted to explain that what he had drawn was a caricature and was not meant to be insulting. Dustin was a cartoonist for the school newspaper. He hoped to have a career someday drawing editorial cartoons for a major newspaper.

Mrs. Blount held up her hand to silence him. "Since you have so much time to draw cartoons," she continued, "I'm assuming you already know how to do the problems we're working on. Please proceed to the chalkboard and show the class how to do number seven."

Dustin hadn't done his geometry homework over the weekend. Actually, Dustin had no idea *how* to do the assignment. He had planned to give it another shot before school that morning. Unfortunately, Dustin always had a hard time getting up on Mondays, and he had overslept.

Dustin raised his hand. If only he could make Mrs. Blount understand that he did caricatures of *everybody*, including his parents, his brother and sister, even the priest at his church. Father Frawley kept his caricature in the rectory and delightedly showed it to everybody who came in. Dustin thought he'd made Father Frawley look much funnier than Mrs. Blount. "Mrs. Blount, I didn't mean to insult you with my drawing," Dustin said.

"Insult?" Mrs. Blount said in mock surprise. "Why would I be insulted? Just because you made me look like some kind of wild animal?" Her face darkened. "Now get out of your seat and show us how brilliant you are."

Dustin felt his face grow warm with embarrassment. He inched out of his seat and stood up, slouching to minimize his size. He had always been tall—too tall, in his opinion. By seventh grade, he had reached almost six feet while the other boys stood barely over five. Now, as a sophomore, there were a couple of kids close to his height of 6' 4" but not many. For the most part, Dustin stood out in a crowd no matter how much he slouched. His father was always nagging him to stand up straight. He had even suggested a few times that Dustin take advantage of his height and go out for the high school basketball team. But Dustin wasn't the basketball type and preferred to remain inconspicuous.

Dustin looked at the jumble of angles and letters on the board. It might as well have been Greek. "Um, I don't exactly remember how to do that problem, Mrs. Blount," he stammered. Several students chuckled.

"I see. Well, then, we'll just substitute this one," Mrs. Blount said, writing another problem on the board. "Go ahead and solve it."

Dustin looked at the problem. There was no way he could decipher it. "Mrs. Blount, I can't do that problem either," he admitted. More laughter.

"Try, Mr. Brand," the teacher urged, her eyes gleaming. Dustin could tell she was enjoying this. She probably saw it as a fit punishment for what he had done. Mrs. Blount was an excellent teacher, and she even had a compassionate side. She would tutor struggling students who really wanted to learn. But she was very stern and wouldn't tolerate any nonsense in her class. Dustin knew the caricature had probably reminded her (and the rest of the class) of her less-than-perfect features. He figured he'd be lucky if she ever forgave him.

"I'm sorry, Mrs. Blount, but I don't know where to begin," Dustin said. "I, um, didn't understand the assignment very well."

"Oh, now, Dustin. I know you understand this. Otherwise, you'd have come in
early this morning for help—and you
didn't, *did you?*" she asked accusingly.
"Now, look at it again!"

As Dustin stood staring blankly at the
chalkboard, a few of the students chuckled, but some began to look uncomfort-
able. It had gone on a bit too long,
and Mrs. Blount was coming across as
sadistic.

Finally Basma Saad, a student from
Iraq, raised her hand.

"Yes, Basma?" Mrs. Blount asked sweet-
ly. Basma was very bright in geometry.

"Mrs. Blount," Basma began. "I think
maybe someone else should do the
problem now, don't you? Could I help
Dustin?"

The smile vanished from Mrs. Blount's
face. "Excuse me, Miss Saad, but I *am* the
teacher in this class, aren't I?"

"Yes, ma'am," Basma said quietly,
lowering her eyes. "But now I think you
are not teaching."

"Miss Saad," the teacher said coldly.

"You are being impudent! You will see me after class." She turned her glaring face toward Dustin. "As for you, Mr. Brand, now that the class has witnessed your incompetence, you may return to your seat. You will also see me after class."

As Dustin sat down, he glanced at the dark-eyed, dark-haired girl who had come to his defense. He had often admired Basma from afar but had never had the nerve to talk to her. He remembered letting her go ahead of him in the cafeteria line sometimes. But that was something he did for any girl, as long as the line wasn't too long or he wasn't too hungry. Now he gave Basma a grateful smile and thought how sorry he was that she'd gotten into trouble because of him.

When class ended, Dustin and Basma approached Mrs. Blount's desk. For a final time, Dustin tried to explain the caricature incident. "I'm really sorry if I offended you but—"

"Enough," Mrs. Blount said, cutting him off. "You will both report to this room after school and spend an hour doing maintenance work on the desks. You're dismissed."

Basma frowned and followed Dustin out of the classroom.

"What does that mean—maintenance work?" Basma asked.

"It probably means we get to clean the gum off the desks," Dustin said. "Hey, Basma, I'm really sorry you got mixed up in this, but thanks anyway."

Basma smiled, her red lips revealing shining white teeth. Dustin thought she looked like Princess Jasmine from *Aladdin*. "Oh, I don't mind too much staying after school. My family owns a gift shop, and when I get out of school, I just have to go to work there, so it's okay."

"Where's your gift shop?" Dustin asked. He was finding it easy to talk to her.

"Across from City Park," Basma answered.

"Maybe I'll come shopping there sometime," Dustin said.

Just then Mark Huber, another student from geometry class, walked up. Mark was a good-looking boy whose family had a lot of money, but Dustin had never liked him much. Dustin could never put his finger on it, but Mark always seemed somewhat sneaky. No matter how friendly Mark tried to be, there always seemed to be an ulterior motive to his friendliness.

Dustin remembered Mark's tenth birthday party. Every student from the fourth grade had been invited. Dustin couldn't figure out why Mark would invite all 52 kids to his party since most kids only invited 6 or 8 of their good friends. But when Dustin got to Mark's house and saw the mountain of gifts stacked in the living room, he understood why. Mark was looking at those gifts as if they were gold. Then he ignored all but a few of the kids at the party. It didn't matter that Mark already had every toy a child could dream of—he wanted more.

Now Mark wedged himself between Dustin and Basma, purposely turning his back to Dustin.

"Hi, Basma," he said. "I'll walk you to your next class."

Basma shrugged her shoulders and said, "Okay." As she headed off with Mark, she called over her shoulder, "I will see you after school tonight, Dustin."

"Yeah, sure," Dustin said. As he watched the two head down the hall, he saw Mark casually drape his arm around Basma's shoulder. Dustin couldn't help wondering why wealthy, good-looking Mark wasn't with his regular crowd of snobby friends.

Dustin's next class was journalism. His job was to create cartoons for the monthly edition of the City High *Sentinel*. His cartoons often featured people from the school and were very popular with the students. Sometimes he used his cartoons to call attention to serious problems, such as drug use or vandalism.

As Dustin entered Mr. Alstead's room, he spotted Joel Riggs already hard at work on the next edition of the *Sentinel*. Joel was the editor of the paper and a pretty fair linebacker on the football team. He liked the cartoons Dustin did of him, even though Dustin made his head too small and his shoulders huge. Dustin sat down beside Joel and told him what had happened in geometry. "Man, I thought I was a goner, Joel," he said. "Mrs. Blount about went ballistic."

"That lady hasn't got a funny bone in her body," Joel said, shaking his head. "I don't think I've ever seen her laugh."

"I just wish she could understand that caricatures are *supposed* to exaggerate a person's features," Dustin said. "That's what makes them work. Anyway, I got an hour's detention with her after school today."

"Gum choppin' time, huh?" Joel said knowingly.

"Yeah, but it's not all bad news," Dustin said. "Basma Saad stood up for me in class, so she's got detention too. At least we'll be working together. Maybe I can get to know her a little better."

"Be careful, man," Joel warned. "I know another guy who was interested in her, and her brother put an end to that real quick. That's a whole different culture there."

Dustin shrugged. "It's not like I'm going to ask her out—at least not right away. I'd just like to be friends with her. Eat lunch with her, stuff like that."

"Just watch yourself, Dustin," Joel said, chuckling. "I'd hate to have you beheaded by an angry brother or uncle."

2 Dustin and Basma reported to Mrs. Blount promptly after school. The teacher was waiting at her desk. She handed each of them a scraping tool. "I expect you to spend the next hour cleaning gum off these desks," she said. From the tone of her voice, Dustin could tell that she was still angry. "I'll be back to inspect them before you leave. I would suggest you not waste any time—or I'll have you back in here tomorrow afternoon!"

When Mrs. Blount left, Dustin and Basma turned over the first row of desks. "I really am sorry, Basma," Dustin said.

"I told you, it's okay," Basma replied. "She was being unjust. I felt I had to speak up."

They began chipping away at multicolored globs of gum. "This is disgusting," Dustin said. "Makes me want to give up chewing gum!"

"Me too," Basma agreed.

"Why don't kids just throw their gum in the wastebasket?" Dustin wondered aloud.

"Then Mrs. Blount would have no ugly

job for us to do," Basma said with a giggle. "She might make us clean pigeon droppings off the bleachers instead."

"Wouldn't surprise me," Dustin said. "Man, she's something else. She can be so strict."

"That is true," Basma said, scraping away. "But she can also be very nice. When I first started here, I was very good at geometry but not so good at English. She let me take tests in a different way. She read me the word problems and explained what they meant. So you see, she has a good side too."

Dustin smiled. "That's nice," he said. "The way you see the good side of people, I mean."

Basma shrugged. "It's not hard if you look," she said.

"You're probably right," Dustin said as he dislodged a huge gob of blue gum. "But she always seems to get on my case. I'm not very good at geometry, as you could probably tell today."

"Oh, I love geometry," Basma said.

"I'm more interested in art," said Dustin. "Actually in cartoons, to be exact."

"I've seen the cartoons you do for the newspaper," Basma said. "They are very good. By the way, if you need help in geometry, I would be glad to work with you."

"Thanks, Basma," Dustin said. He felt good. She was being so nice to him. Maybe she wouldn't reject him the way other girls did. He took a deep breath. "Basma, maybe we could eat lunch together tomorrow. We have the same lunch shift."

"We do?" Basma asked. "I guess I never noticed. All right, Dustin. I will eat lunch with you. I'm bringing *baklava* tomorrow."

"Who's *baklava?*" Dustin asked, thinking it might be the overprotective brother Joel had mentioned.

Basma laughed. "Not *who*, silly—*what*. *Baklava* is a pastry from my country. It's made of nuts and honey and is very good. I will bring an extra piece for you. You'll see."

"Sounds good," Dustin said. For the next half an hour, they worked in silence. Dustin couldn't believe what a hard worker Basma was. He was sure by the end of the hour that Basma had cleaned more desks than he had. "Do you always work this hard?" he asked.

Basma shrugged. "I'm used to it," she said. "In my country, if you don't work, you don't survive."

"How long have you been in the United States?" Dustin asked.

"Only one year," Basma said.

"Well, I'm glad you came," Dustin said.

At 4:20, Mrs. Blount walked in. She inspected Dustin and Basma's work in grim silence. Then with a wave of her hand, she dismissed them.

"Whew," Dustin said when they were outside. "I'm glad that's over." A cool mist was falling, and the wind had come up. "Guess I'd better do my assignment tonight, huh? How do you get home?"

"I walk," Basma said. "My brother doesn't allow me to ride the bus. He says there are troublemakers on the bus who will say rude things."

Dustin nodded toward the parking lot, where his rusty, banged-up van sat. It was all Dustin could afford. His parents had purchased the van for him, but he was expected to pay the insurance by working at the local supermarket a few hours per week. "Why don't I give you a lift? It's the least I can do after what you did for me. Besides, it's raining."

"Okay," Basma said.

As they climbed into the van, Dustin noticed Mark Huber in the distance. This time he was with his usual crowd—Kimberly Cross, Emma Lorenzo, and a couple of other kids from wealthy families. They were laughing and talking as they headed toward their fancy cars. As Dustin and Basma were getting in the van, Mark spotted them.

"Hey, Basma," he called as he approached the van. "What are you doing getting into that old rust bucket?"

"Dustin is giving me a ride to the gift shop," Basma answered.

"You sure you want to ride in that thing?" Mark laughed. "I can give you a ride." He pointed at his shiny new sports car.

"No, thank you," Basma said.

Mark shrugged and walked away. "Suit yourself," he said, rejoining his friends. As Dustin and Basma left the lot, Dustin could see the group laughing and pointing at his van.

"So what's going on between you and Mark?" Dustin asked, remembering how Mark had put his arm around Basma earlier that day.

"Nothing," Basma said curtly. "He's just a friend."

Dustin would have liked to know more, but he let it go. If Basma didn't want to talk about Mark, she must not be too crazy about him, he told himself. At least he hoped that was the way it was.

As they neared the gift shop, Dustin slowed down. Remembering her brother, Dustin said, "You want me to drop you off a little before the store so your brother—"

"No!" Basma said, her eyes flashing. "I have done nothing wrong. Why should my brother be upset? I will say to him, 'You want I should get wet and ruin my clothes?' He knows we can't afford new clothes for me."

"He sounds more like a father than a brother," Dustin remarked.

Basma nodded. "My papa died when I was very young," she said. "Since then my brother thinks he is the head of the family. I respect my brother, but when he gets mad for no reason, I tell him he's wrong."

Dustin smiled and remembered how Basma had stood up to Mrs. Blount earlier that day. "Does he listen to you?" he asked.

"No, but I don't care. He thinks because he is the oldest son, he knows everything. He is not my papa, but he thinks he has the right to boss me. I tell him I do what I want."

As Dustin pulled up to the curb in front of the gift shop, he saw a slender dark-skinned young man arranging figurines in the display window. "Is that your brother?" Dustin asked.

"Yes, that's Nazar," Basma said. As she got out of the van, Nazar came out of the store and glared at her.

"What is going on?" he asked accusingly.

"I'm in Basma's geometry class," Dustin explained. "I offered her a ride home because it's raining."

Nazar looked at Dustin with the coldest eyes Dustin had ever seen. "I am not talking to you, *dude*," he said. He spit the last word out as if it were a piece of rotten apple. Then he reached out and grabbed Basma's hand. "Go into the store," he commanded. "You are late!"

Basma wrenched herself free of her brother's grasp. "I did nothing wrong, Nazar!" she said. Then, turning back to Dustin, she said, "Thanks for the ride home, Dustin."

"Anytime," Dustin said. Then he turned to Nazar. "Hey, look, I just gave her a ride home. It's no big deal. Really."

"No, *you* look, *dude,*" Nazar sneered. "Stay away from my sister. She's not one of your typical American bimbos, you got that?"

"Calm down, buddy," Dustin said. "For your information, all American girls are not bimbos."

"I am not your buddy," Nazar said. "Just don't try to take advantage of my sister!"

Dustin sighed. If this guy weren't so nasty, he would almost be funny, he thought. "I have no intentions of taking advantage of anyone," he said. "Besides, Basma is a real smart girl. No one is going to take advantage of her."

Nazar laughed. "She's smart, but she is still a girl! Girls are foolish and weak. That is why they need protection. That is what I am here for. Just remember that, *dude.*"

3 "Why are you so late, honey?" Mrs. Brand asked when Dustin got home.

"I got detention, Mom," Dustin said.

"Detention?" echoed his younger sister, Becky. She was sitting at the kitchen table doing her homework. "I love it! You never get detention."

"What did you do to get detention?" Dustin's mother asked.

"I drew a caricature of Mrs. Blount in geometry. I didn't mean for her to see it, but she did. Boy, was she mad!" He didn't mention the part about not doing the assignment.

Becky covered her mouth with her hand to stifle her laughter, but his mother frowned at him. "Dustin, you know better than that," she said.

"Mom, I hate geometry," Dustin protested. "I'll never be good at it. But if I practice my caricatures, maybe someday I'll be good enough to get a job doing them. I won't need geometry then."

Dustin's father appeared in the doorway. He had been working on the computer in the den and had heard the conversation.

"I can't believe this," he said. "You were drawing silly pictures of your teacher instead of working? Dustin, you're almost seventeen years old. When are you going to grow up and stop that silly doodling?"

Dustin could feel his stomach tightening as it always did when the subject of his cartoons came up between him and his father. He took a deep breath. "Dad," he said, "my silly doodling might just turn out to be my career someday. Other people have made careers at being cartoonists. Look at Thomas Nast. He's in our history books. He drew political cartoons that were so powerful, they helped change the course of history."

Mr. Brand sighed. "Dustin, have you read the latest studies on the types of jobs that will be in demand in the 21st century?" Dustin's father was a counselor at the local community college and was very up-to-date on employment studies. "Well, I have. And believe me, cartoonists are not even on the list. The world is going to need engineers, computer technicians, medical personnel—not cartoonists. It's fine if you want to fiddle around with drawing pictures in your spare time, although I'd prefer you did something worthwhile, like basketball. But it really bothers me that you're getting into trouble during an important class like geometry because you're doodling instead of paying attention."

"Okay, Dad, I hear you," Dustin said wearily. He felt like covering his ears, but he knew better.

"No, that's the trouble," his father continued. "You don't hear me. You're not taking life seriously, son."

"Dad, that's just what I *am* doing," Dustin protested. "The better I get at cartooning, the better chance I'll have of breaking into the field someday."

"Field?" Mr. Brand asked. "Cartooning is a field? Dustin, accounting is a field, engineering is a field. Cartooning is, well, cartooning. Think about it. It's kid stuff. Only a few people really make it big in cartooning. You'd better stick to something more realistic—something you'll have a chance of succeeding at."

Dustin gave up. He knew from previous experience that his dad was beyond reasoning with when he put himself in his counselor mode. Dustin escaped to his room and sat in the big chair in the corner, the only chair in the house comfortable enough for his lanky frame. Becky was tall for her age, but she was still only five 5' 8". Even his father was only 5' 10". Which is why, Dustin thought, he wants me to go out for basketball so bad. Dustin's father had been a good ball handler in high school, but he just didn't have the height to make first string. Dustin knew that Mr. Brand was trying to grab the glory he never got by urging his 6' 4" son to play.

Dustin had played basketball in junior high and was really pretty good. The high school coach had come to some of the games and tried to recruit him for the next year. But, while Dustin liked basketball, he had no interest in playing it day and night, which is what he'd end up doing if he made the high school team.

Instead, Dustin had gotten interested in art. He'd had an outstanding art teacher in ninth grade who had encouraged him to enter contests. He'd won several second-

and third-place awards and even one first-place. Now as he sat in his chair, he glanced up at the ribbons proudly displayed on his bulletin board in his room. He wished his parents were as proud of his accomplishments as he was. But they seemed to place more stock in academics and sports.

Dustin's older brother Doug was an engineer at a big plastics company. His academic awards from high school and college were displayed all over the house. Becky was an outstanding basketball player. In fact, even though she was only in eighth grade, she'd already received some attention from both state universities about playing at that level. Dustin's parents had her team pictures and trophies in the bookcase in the entryway. But there were very few signs of Dustin's accomplishments in the house.

"We're just waiting for the right award, the one that really shows your talents," Mrs. Brand had once told Dustin. "It'll come one of these days, and when it does, we'll put it on the fireplace mantel for everyone to see." Dustin doubted if that day would ever come.

Dustin got up and went to his desk. He began sketching the cartoon for this month's issue of the City High *Sentinel*. Often he didn't have a definite plan for the cartoon, just an idea. He would sit down and let his fingers start drawing, never sure what the end product would be. But more often than not, he would be pleased with what he had done. Dustin had a natural talent for cartooning; he was sure of that. And no matter what his dad said, he was going to continue to develop that talent. His cartoons allowed him to escape to a world where he was in control. And he liked that world a lot, sometimes more than the real world he lived in.

* * *

On Tuesday, Dustin's journalism teacher, who was also the advisor for the *Sentinel*, stopped Dustin in the hall before first period. "Exciting news, Dustin!" Mr. Alstead began. "I just found out about a new award that's out this year for high school cartoonists—the Hogarth award. Evidently, it's going to be an annual thing.

It's in honor of William Hogarth, the fellow from England who drew cartoons in the 1700s."

Dustin's interest was piqued. "What do the cartoons have to be about?" he asked.

"Entries have to be based on everyday life in the classroom," Mr. Alstead said. "You know, something students from all over the country can relate to. I thought I'd tell you about it now so you'd have a chance to create a really good cartoon for next week's edition of the *Sentinel.* All entries are due the following week, and they have to be published before they can be submitted."

"Do you think I've got a chance, Mr. Alstead?" Dustin asked.

"I do, indeed," Mr. Alstead said with a wink. "And it's worth a thousand dollars to you—that's part of the award!"

A thousand dollars! Just for drawing a cartoon? Dustin felt a new spring to his step as he headed toward his first class. Ideas for new cartoons swirled in his head like leaves in a windstorm. He was so eager to get some solid recognition for his cartooning—something to show his father.

Dustin looked for Basma at lunch. He was a little nervous that maybe she'd forgotten that they were planning on eating together. But when he approached her table, she looked up and smiled. "I brought the *baklava* I promised. Here's a piece for you."

Dustin sat down and took a bite. "This is great," he raved. "Did you make it?"

"No, Mama did, but I helped her."

Then Dustin told Basma about the Hogarth award. "It sounds very exciting," she said. "What would you win?"

"A thousand dollars!" Dustin said. "And I'd probably get some recognition, like in the local newspaper."

"That's wonderful!" said Basma. "Good luck!"

"Say, Basma," Dustin said, taking another bite of the rich, flaky dessert, "you said you'd give me some help in geometry. Maybe you could ride home with me today, and we could spend some time working on it. I'm really behind. I think I need to review the whole chapter."

"Sure," Basma said with a grin. "I would be glad to help you."

"It won't get you in trouble with your brother, will it?" Dustin asked.

Basma's dark eyes sparked. "My brother! I told him he better quit making hassles with my friends. He thinks he's a big shot because he goes to the university. But I'm smarter than he is. I will also go to the university and do better than he does!"

"I wouldn't be surprised if you did," said Dustin.

Lunch period passed too quickly. When the bell rang for fifth period, Dustin said, "So I'll meet you in the parking lot, okay? You know what my van looks like."

"Okay," Basma answered. "See you after school."

After school, Dustin and Basma went to Dustin's house. His father was in the den working on his computer.

"Dad, this is my friend, Basma, from school," Dustin said. "She's a real geometry whiz, and she's going to help me for a while."

"It's nice to meet you, Basma," Mr. Brand said politely. Dustin noticed that his father's greeting seemed to be more automatic than sincere.

Dustin and Basma began by reviewing the section on bisecting angles. Basma pointed out a few quick ways to divide an angle in two.

"Oh, man," Dustin said. "The way you explain it makes so much sense."

"Geometry isn't hard," Basma explained. "You just have to look at it logically."

"I guess I'm not a very logical person," Dustin said. At least that's what my dad thinks, he thought.

"Okay, now let's see how you do on tomorrow's assignment," Basma said. "I won't help you unless you ask."

Dustin spent the next fifteen minutes working on the five problems. He was thrilled that he only had to ask Basma for help once. "This has been great, Basma," he said as he finished. "You've been a big help."

Basma smiled at him and said, "I enjoyed it, Dustin."

Suddenly Dustin felt very close to her. She was easy to talk to and seemed to like being with him.

"Unfortunately," Basma added, "I have

to go to the gift shop now. My family needs my help. We were supposed to get a big shipment in this afternoon, and I have to help unpack it and put it on the shelves."

"No problem," Dustin said, taking out his keys. "Let's go."

Dustin drove Basma to the gift shop. Luckily, Nazar wasn't glaring at him from the front door this time.

"Thanks again for helping me, Basma," Dustin said as Basma got out of the van.

"You're welcome, Dustin," Basma said. "It was fun."

"Can we eat lunch together again tomorrow?" Dustin asked.

"Sure," said Basma. "See you then."

As Dustin drove home, he found himself looking forward to going to school the next day. He told himself that after a few lunches, maybe he could muster up the courage to ask Basma out.

When Dustin returned home, his father was waiting for him at the kitchen table.

"Dustin, I'd like a word with you," Mr. Brand said.

Oh, boy, what'd I do now? Dustin

wondered. Reluctantly he sat down across from his father.

"That girl, Basma," his father began. "Where's she from?"

Dustin hesitated. "Iraq," he finally said.

"Mmm, pretty girl," Mr. Brand said. "There's quite a lot of them around the city—people from Iraq, I mean. They're a different lot, that's for sure."

"What do you mean, Dad?" Dustin asked.

"Well, you know, their culture. It's a lot different from ours, don't you think?"

Dustin shrugged. "I don't know. They work hard for a living just like we do. What are you getting at, Dad?"

"Well, son, I just think it's fine that Basma is helping you with your geometry," Mr. Brand said. "Heaven knows you need all the help you can get. But I wouldn't get too involved with her."

"Dad, who said anything about getting involved?" Dustin asked. "Basma's just helping me with my geometry."

Mr. Brand laughed dryly. "Come on, son. You're a young, healthy boy, and she's a very pretty girl."

Dustin sighed. He could feel his mind start to turn off as usual. He said, "Dad, right now Basma's just a classmate. I don't know if it will develop into something more than that. But if it does, I hope I don't have to ask your permission. Because that's the way *her* family does it—and they're different from us, remember?"

"Watch your tone of voice, young man," Mr. Brand warned. "I'm only looking out for your own good."

"So you think I'm too stupid to choose good friends?" Dustin asked. He was starting to get angry now.

"I didn't say that. But I *am* older than you, and, believe it or not, I have learned a few things. I just thought you might benefit from my advice."

"Look, Dad, I know you're just trying to help," Dustin said. "But trust me on this, okay? Let me at least choose the few friends I have."

"Okay, son," Mr. Brand said. "But you know, if you went out for basketball, you'd probably have a lot more friends. Good athletes are very popular. Just ask Becky."

"I'm not sure I want any more friends,

Dad," Dustin said. "Especially if the only reason they like me is because I can stuff a ball through a hoop." Dustin turned abruptly and went to his room. He felt frustrated with the conversation he'd had with his father and decided to work off his anger by sketching some new cartoons. He quickly sketched a teacher in a fetal position under his desk, clutching a teddy bear. Another teacher was walking by saying, "Tough fifth period, eh, Klosterman?" Dustin smiled and then began sketching a few more ideas. He was pleased with his efforts and wanted to share the cartoons with someone who would appreciate them. He glanced at the clock. If he left for the gift shop now, he could show the cartoons to Basma and be back in time for dinner.

Dustin jumped into his van and drove to the gift shop. As he hurried into the store, he glanced around for Basma. He spotted her at the cash register.

"Hey, Basma," he said as he approached. "I did these today. What do you think?" He handed her his sketches.

Basma laughed out loud at the teacher

and the teddy bear. "This is great!" she said. "I guess sometimes we make the poor teachers crazy like they make us, eh?"

"No kidding," Dustin agreed. "So you like them?"

"They're very good, Dustin," Basma said. "You have a lot of talent."

"Thanks," Dustin said. "I'm going to polish them up and think of some more tonight. I'll see you tomorrow."

Dustin headed toward the door. Two girls from City High had entered the shop as Dustin and Basma were talking. Dustin recognized them as Kimberly Cross and Emma Lorenzo. He hadn't paid much attention to the girls until now when they rushed past him as he left the store. Then he heard a woman shout, "Basma! Two of the musical birthday cards are gone from the display!"

Dustin was already out the door when Mrs. Saad came hurrying toward him, her face flushed with anger.

4 Mrs. Saad looked suspiciously at Dustin. "You are from the high school?" she asked.

"Yes, ma'am," Dustin said.

"Mama," Basma said as she joined her mother. "I didn't see anyone steal anything."

"Do you know this boy?" Mrs. Saad asked.

"Yes, he's my friend," Basma answered.

"You were with the two girls who came in here?" the older woman asked.

"No, ma'am," Dustin answered.

"Mama!" Basma protested.

"Hush!" Mrs. Saad said. "You were talking to this boy when you were supposed to be minding the store. How do we know he did not plan it that way?"

Narrowing her eyes, she turned back to Dustin. "We have many students from the high school in here every day, and always something turns up missing. Often one student gets our attention while another fills his pockets. Already this month we have had two expensive necklaces and a crystal paperweight stolen!"

"Mrs. Saad," Dustin said. "I didn't come

here to shoplift. I was only showing Basma some of my sketches."

"Mama, please. . ." Basma began. A sharp glance from her mother stopped Basma from protesting.

"This time I will let you go," Mrs. Saad said. "Next time will not be so easy! Come, Basma!"

"I'm really sorry, Dustin," Basma said. "I'll see you tomorrow." She headed back into the store with her mother.

"It's okay," Dustin said. "See you tomorrow."

Dustin felt sorry for Basma and her family. He hated the fact that a few students from City High stole from them. He thought it must be hard enough to make it in a new country without being ripped off by the locals.

* * *

As Dustin headed for geometry the next day, he found himself looking forward to seeing Basma again. But when he entered the room, he saw Mark Huber turned around in his chair talking to her. Disappointed, Dustin walked to his desk on the other side of the room. As he sat down, he noticed Kimberly Cross talking to a girl behind her.

"Look at the cute birthday card I got for Pete," Kimberly was saying. "Listen." She opened the card, and Dustin listened as it played "Happy Birthday."

"Oh, wow," the girl said. "That is so cool. Where'd you get them?"

"At the gift shop across from the park," Kimberly said. "Look, I got two of them. They were so cool I wanted them both."

Dustin winced. *Two* musical birthday cards. He was pretty sure it wasn't a coincidence that Kimberly had been in the Saads' gift shop when the cards disappeared.

After geometry, Dustin approached Kimberly. "I heard your birthday card," he said amiably. "That's a great idea. Where did you say you got them? I want to buy one for my mom."

"Oh, down at that little gift shop across from City Park," Kimberly answered.

"How much were they?" Dustin asked.

A strange look came over Kimberly's face. "I forget," she said.

"Maybe you've still got the sales slip in your purse," Dustin suggested. "I'd like to see how much they are before I head over there. I'm a little short on cash right now."

"Oh, I never keep receipts," Kimberly said. "Sorry, but I've to get to class." She started to walk away.

"Kimberly," Dustin said, lowering his voice. "I was at the gift shop yesterday when somebody ripped off two of those cards. I could have sworn I saw you in the shop then."

"Hey, what are you getting at?" Kimberly demanded.

"I just feel bad that kids from City High are stealing from the family that owns that store," Dustin said. "It makes the rest of us look like thieves too."

"I don't know where you get off accusing me of stealing, Dustin Brand," Kimberly said, her eyes flashing with anger. "But it seems to me that a lot of those foreigners rip *us* off by charging such high prices for their stuff."

"Kim, that's not true, and you know it," Dustin said. "They're just trying to make a living. And they don't need—" But before he could say any more, Kimberly stomped off toward her next class.

Dustin shook his head. He doubted that he'd gotten through to her.

As he entered journalism class, Dustin put Kimberly out of his mind. Mr. Alstead was at his desk, and Dustin was anxious to show him his latest sketches.

"These are good, Dustin," Mr. Alstead said after looking over the cartoons. "Very good. With this kind of work, I think you've got a good chance at that award. You know, winning the Hogarth would not only be great for you, but it would also be a real boost to the school—particularly the journalism department."

Not to mention the boost it would give me in my dad's eyes, Dustin thought. "I'll keep working on them," Dustin said.

Later at lunch, Dustin found Basma sitting at the same table as the day before. She smiled as he approached.

"Basma, I'm really sorry about the trouble with your mom yesterday," he said.

Basma rolled her eyes. "Mama thinks I should have eyes in the back of my head," Basma said. "But I don't want to talk about yesterday. How are your sketches coming?"

"Real well," Dustin said. "Mr. Alstead thinks I've got a good shot at the Hogarth."

"That's wonderful, Dustin," Basma said. "So you're going to be a cartoonist when you grow up?"

"I hope so," Dustin said. "That is, if my dad doesn't talk me into being an accountant or a computer programmer or something. What do you want to be?"

"I will become a scientist," Basma said resolutely. "Maybe a biologist, and I'll do research on diseases. I'd like to cure something, like cancer or AIDS. Then I'd be remembered for doing something good."

"That's a pretty noble ambition," Dustin said with admiration. "A lot more noble than mine."

"No, no," Basma said. "That's not true. The world needs scientists, but it also needs humor. It's important that people laugh to forget the sad things. So we both have great things to do with our lives, eh?"

"Thanks," Dustin said. "I only wish my

parents felt that way, especially my dad." He realized that he was really beginning to like Basma. She had such a down-to-earth way of looking at things, and he'd never met a girl who was so easy to talk to. Maybe she would go out with him. "Do you like the movies, Basma?" he asked.

"Not really," Basma said. "I have a hard time relating to them. Everything is too perfect."

"What *do* you like to do, then?" asked Dustin.

"I like to do things outdoors," Basma said. "Like walk in the desert or by the seashore. I like to see the plants that grow in those places. I'm doing my science project on desert plants."

"Well, maybe this coming Saturday, we could drive out to the edge of the desert," Dustin said. "It's only about two hours away. We could spend a couple of hours walking around and then maybe have a picnic lunch. Would you like that?"

"Oh, yes," Basma said. "That would be fun. I'll ask my mother tonight. She might say yes if my brother is not there. I could take my camera along and take pictures for my project. And I'll bring some special dishes my mother makes."

"Great," Dustin said, smiling. "I could pick you up about eight, and we could be home by three or so. Now, do you think you could help me with the geometry assignment for tomorrow? I am lost—again!"

* * *

When Dustin got home from school, he told his mother about his plans for Saturday. "If she can come, Basma's bringing some food. I'd like to bring something too. Can you help me?"

"Sure," Mrs. Brand said. "I'll make my famous fried chicken."

"Maybe a chocolate cake too?" Dustin asked.

"Well, if you help me I might have time," his mother answered. "So you like this girl, huh, Dustin?"

Dustin nodded. "She's really nice," he said.

"She's Iraqi, isn't she?" Mrs. Brand asked.

"Um, yeah. . ." Dustin said.

"Their culture is quite strict. Are you

sure her parents will let her go?"

"She doesn't have a father—just a mother and a brother. She's going to ask tonight," Dustin said. "But why shouldn't she? I mean, it's sort of like a science field trip."

"I hope they look at it that way," Mrs. Brand said.

Dustin looked for Basma the minute he got out of his van in the school parking lot on Thursday morning. He spotted her coming down the street, her backpack strapped to her shoulders. He waited for her in front of the building. As she drew closer, Dustin saw that she was upset.

"What's the matter, Basma?" he asked.

"My mother said I can't go with you on Saturday," she said bitterly. "It is so unjust! So unjust!"

"Why not?" Dustin asked. "Was your brother home?'

Basma hesitated. Then, without looking at Dustin, she said, "No, but my mother said that I should not go with someone who might be a thief."

5 Dustin felt like he had been hit with a rock. He didn't know that Mrs. Saad still suspected him of helping Kimberly and Emma. How would she ever let Basma go out with him if she thought he had stolen from them?

"Hey, Basma," he said. "It's okay. We can go to the desert another time."

"Mama thinks too much like Nazar sometimes," Basma said.

"We'll work it out," Dustin said. "I just have to prove to your mother that I'm not a thief."

"But how will you do that?" Basma asked.

"I don't know yet, but I'll figure out something," Dustin said.

What Basma had said bothered Dustin all day. He didn't like the thought of being suspected of shoplifting. He had to do something to prove he wasn't a thief. He pondered the problem all day and while working at the grocery store after school. When he got home that night, he still hadn't thought of a plan.

At 9:00, he sat down to watch his favorite detective show when it came to him. *He* would catch the thieves! He would go to the gift shop after school tomorrow and volunteer to help the Saad family catch whoever was stealing from them. Then they would realize he wasn't a thief and maybe let Basma go to the desert with him.

Dustin felt relieved as he climbed into bed later that night. Maybe things with Basma would work out after all. He fell asleep quickly and slept soundly until about 4:00 a.m. when he awoke with a start. As often happened during the night, an idea for a cartoon was taking shape in his head. He got out of bed, rushed to his desk, and began sketching a classroom full of students. The students were dressed in the popular style at City High: huge, baggy jeans or overalls that dragged on the floor, t-shirts covered by big, sloppy flannel shirts, and ball caps turned backward. Some of the students wore several pierced earrings in each ear, while others had their eyebrows or noses pierced. The hair styles ranged from spiked, rainbow-colored hair to no hair at all. In contrast to the rest of the students, a clean-cut boy was standing at the lectern in front of the class. He was wearing a freshly ironed shirt tucked into pants that actually fit him. His short hair was neatly combed, and the only jewelry he wore was his class ring. The boy was pointing to something on the overhead projector screen. The caption to the cartoon read, "Endangered Species 101 guest lecturers." Waiting to speak next were a mountain gorilla, a Bengal tiger, and a spotted owl.

Dustin laughed out loud. Grandpa would have liked this, he thought. He glanced at the caricature of his grandfather that hung above his desk. Dustin had drawn it a few months before his grandfather died. It was a good likeness of the older man's face, complete with his twinkling eyes and huge smile. Dustin had seen that smile many times, especially when he showed his grandfather his cartoons. His grandfather would take the drawings into his big hands, guffaw loudly, and say, "Good job, Dusty. Keep it up. They're getting funnier all the time."

Dustin missed the old man's encouragement and wished desperately that his own father would approve of his interest in cartooning. Just then his father poked his head in the door.

"What in the world are you doing, Dustin?" his father asked. "I got up to get a drink of water, and I heard you laughing in here."

"Dad," Dustin said, still excited about his cartoon. "I got this idea for a cartoon, and it just couldn't wait. I was afraid I'd forget it by morning."

"I guess I should have known better than to think you'd be up studying," Mr. Brand said dryly. "I can't believe you get up in the middle of the night to draw cartoons. Now go back to bed. You're going to have the whole household awake!"

"But, Dad," Dustin continued. "There's this national contest for high school cartoonists Mr. Alstead told me about. It's called the Hogarth award. If I could win it—"

"Dustin, losing sleep over a cartoon is ridiculous," Dad said. "I've told you before to put your efforts into something that'll do you some good. Now go back to bed." With that, he closed Dustin's door.

Dustin sank back down on his bed. He felt as if the wind had been taken from his sails. Ever since he was a small boy, he had fantasized about doing something great to impress his father. At first, Dustin thought he might become a world-class athlete, even a gold medalist at the Olympics. He saw himself bowing slightly as the medal was placed around his neck and the national anthem played. His father would be in the audience, smiling proudly as if to say, "Way to go, son." But Dustin had little interest in sports, so he knew *that* dream would never become a reality.

At other times, Dustin imagined bringing home a report card that would blow his dad away—all A's! But he knew that no matter how hard he worked, he'd never be more than an average student. But if he could win the Hogarth, then he'd have something tangible to show his father. Maybe the school would have some sort of assembly, and he would be presented with a framed award and a check for a thousand dollars. Then his dad couldn't help but be impressed.

Dustin made up his mind right then and

there that he would do whatever it took to win the award. Somehow he had to show his dad that his talents as a cartoonist were something to be admired, not scoffed at.

* * *

After school the next day, Dustin went to the gift shop. As he entered the store, he spotted Basma at the cash register.

"Hi, Basma," he whispered as he approached the counter. He glanced around. "Is your brother here?"

"No, he's at the university," Basma said.

Just then Mrs. Saad came out of the storeroom behind the counter. She cast an unfriendly look in Dustin's direction and said, "So, you want to buy something today, eh?"

"Mrs. Saad," Dustin began. "I'm really sorry about the kids who come in here and shoplift. I thought maybe today I could hang around the shop for an hour or so. This is the time they usually come in, isn't it?"

Mrs. Saad nodded but didn't say anything.

"Anyway, I've brought some sketches along, so I thought I'd sit over there in the corner and work on them. Then I can kind of keep an eye on the kids who come in. Maybe I can spot whoever is stealing from you. They won't suspect me."

Mrs. Saad looked more suspicious and unfriendly than ever. "Nobody asked you to do this. What do you want?" she demanded.

"Nothing, Mrs. Saad. Really," Dustin assured her. "Basma has helped me with my geometry a couple of times. This is just my way of saying thanks."

Abruptly Basma's mother turned her back on Dustin and went back into the storeroom. Basma smiled. "That means it's all right," she said. "Show me your sketches."

Basma grinned as she looked at each cartoon. When she got to the endangered species cartoon, she giggled and said, "This is really good, Dustin. I like this one best."

"I like it too," Dustin said. "I left a copy of it with Mr. Alstead today, but I haven't had a chance to talk to him about it. Well,

I guess I'll work over here."

Dustin retired to a small table and chair in the corner. On top of the table was a mirror and a display of necklaces and earrings. Dustin assumed that customers sat at the table to try on the jewelry and see how it looked in the mirror.

A few minutes later, three girls from City High came into the shop. Dustin recognized them as being part of Mark Huber and Kimberly Cross's group. The girls paid no attention to him. Two of them headed for the aisle with the fine chocolates, and the third girl went up to the cash register where Basma was standing. She began asking Basma about the crystal window decorations in a case next to the cash register.

Dustin pretended to be absorbed in his sketches. He listened as he heard the two girls whispering one aisle over.

"Oh, Teal, I just love these truffles, don't you?" one girl asked.

"Are you kidding?" Teal answered. "I could eat a whole box."

"You get one too, then," the first girl said. "I'll get these pecan turtles for Ellen."

"Good idea," said Teal.

Dustin could hear purses zipping open and shut. Then he saw the girls approach the cash register.

"You ready to go, El?" one of them asked. "We are."

"Yeah, I guess so," Ellen answered. Then she said to Basma, "I guess I'll get one of those crystals another time. But thanks for your help."

The three headed for the door. Dustin got up from the table and met them as they came down the aisle.

"You girls like chocolate, huh?" he asked.

"Sure, who doesn't," the girl who was in the aisle with Teal answered.

"You want to pay for those boxes you have in your purses?" Dustin asked. "Or would you rather just put them back? Your choice."

Teal looked frightened. "What's going on?" she demanded. She glanced back at Basma, who had been joined by her mother at the cash register. Mrs. Saad was watching Dustin closely.

"Look," Dustin said. "If you don't have money for the stuff you took, just put it back, okay? No harm done."

Teal and the other girl turned around sharply, opened their purses, and laid the boxes of chocolates on the counter. "There!" the other girl said. "Are you satisfied?"

"Quite," Dustin said. "Have a nice day, ladies."

He glanced at Mrs. Saad. The older woman dropped her eyes, turned away abruptly, and returned to the back room.

"Thank you, Dustin," Basma said. "Those girls have been in here before. I doubt that they will be back."

A few other students came into the shop during the next hour, but they all paid for their purchases. Then Mark Huber came in. He glanced at Dustin and then walked by him as if he didn't exist.

"Hey, babe," he said to Basma as he approached the front counter. He was smiling the disarming smile Dustin had seen him use so often on students as well as teachers. "How's it going?"

Basma looked up. "Fine," she said. She glanced at Dustin and then back at Mark.

"When do you get off?" Mark asked. "I

thought maybe we'd go for a pizza or something."

"Not today, Mark," Basma said, shaking her head. "We're very busy."

Just then Mrs. Saad came out of the back room. To Dustin's surprise, Mrs. Saad said pleasantly, "Hello, Mark."

"Hello, Mrs. Saad," Mark said still smiling. "How are you?" He looked at the older woman as if nothing else in the world mattered at that moment except her well-being.

Mrs. Saad rolled her eyes. "Exhausted," she said. "To run a gift shop is a lot of work."

"Mrs. Saad," Mark began in a sugar-cookie voice. "I was just asking Basma if she wanted to go for pizza. She says she's too busy."

Mrs. Saad frowned at Basma. "You come back in one hour, Mark," she said. "Business dies down over the dinner hour. Basma may go with you then."

"Thank you, Mrs. Saad," Mark said. "See you in an hour, Basma." With a smirk on his face, he glanced at Dustin and then left the store.

Dustin approached Basma when her mother had returned to the storeroom. "Um, Basma," he said hesitantly. "Are you dating Mark Huber or something? I guess I figured your mother didn't like American boys."

Basma shook her head. "I don't want to date Mark. I don't like him. He's too funny." Dustin looked at her questioningly, and she quickly corrected herself. "I mean, phony. But my mother and brother would like me to date him. They don't mind him because they know his family is wealthy."

Dustin felt discouraged and walked back to the corner. Now it would be harder than ever to get Basma's mother and brother to allow Basma to go out with him.

Near the end of the hour, two boys that Dustin didn't recognize came in. One approached Basma at the cash register while the other headed down another aisle.

"Do you have any birthday figurines?" the boy asked Basma. "I need one for my sister's birthday next week."

"Sure, they are in the first aisle," Basma

said pleasantly.

The boy headed down the aisle. A few seconds later, he called, "Miss, the one I want is up too high. Could you get it down for me?"

"I'll be right there," Basma called. She reached under the counter and brought out a small step stool. Then she headed down the first aisle.

Dustin had a feeling that a set-up was underway. While Basma was up on the step stool getting the figurine off the shelf, Dustin went to the far aisle and peeked around the corner. There he saw the first boy putting a fancy cigarette lighter into his pocket. Dustin approached the boy.

"Hey, do you smoke?" Dustin asked. "You know that's bad for your health."

The boy looked at Dustin in surprise and then anger. "What's it to you?" he growled.

"I just think you'd better put that lighter back or pay for it," Dustin said.

"And who are you?"

"Nobody special," Dustin said. "But the guy who owns this place has you on film right now." He pointed to a brown spot on one of the ceiling tiles. "See that spot on the ceiling that looks like a leak? There's a security camera up there pointed right at you."

The boy looked uncertainly at the ceiling, then back at Dustin. Finally, he removed the lighter from his pocket and headed for the cash register. "It was for my dad," he grumbled.

"I'm sure your dad will enjoy it more knowing that you got it honestly," Dustin said. Basma rang up the sale and handed the boy his purchase.

Then Dustin and Basma watched as the boys headed down the street. "Thank you again, Dustin," Basma said. "That's three times you have helped my family."

"No problem," Dustin said. "Maybe now they'll let you go on our little field trip on Saturday."

"Don't bet on it, *dude.*" Dustin turned to see Nazar standing behind him.

6 "I thought I told you to stay away from my sister," Nazar said.

Basma sighed. "Dustin is catching shoplifters, Nazar," she tried to explain. "He's helping us."

"Quiet!" Nazar snapped. "Just what do you want?"

"Basma's right," Dustin began. "I came here today to see if I could find out who's been ripping you off."

"Oh, right," Nazar sneered. "Just out of the goodness of your heart, eh, *dude?*"

"You know what, man?" Dustin said. "I got a name. It's Dustin. D-u-s-t-i-n. You can call me Dustin any time you get as sick of "dude" as I am."

"Look, you're not fooling me for a minute," Nazar said. "You're hanging around here to get in good with my family so you can take my sister out. Well, that has all been settled. My mother and I talked it over. Basma is not dating you, *dude.*" Nazar narrowed his eyes. "We're still not convinced that you're not a thief yourself. Do you know what happens to thieves in my country?" He made a chopping motion with one hand against the other wrist.

Dustin was angry now. He was tired of this paranoid, over-protective character treating him like a criminal. "Well, I'm not in your country now. I'm in the United States. And here a person is innocent until proven guilty."

"You are a smooth-talker, but you're not fooling me," Nazar said. "You remind me of the hyena. He is a cunning, sneaky fellow who takes advantage of the other animals during the day. Then at night, he laughs at the mischief he's gotten away with." He shook his head. "Just so you know, little hyena, you will not be laughing at my sister!"

"I don't plan on laughing at your sister," Dustin said. "And I am not a hyena."

Nazar suddenly came very close to Dustin. He extended his index finger and stuck it into the middle of Dustin's chest for emphasis. "All day at the university I watch the guys and hear them laugh at the way they treat girls. Then, when the girl loses all self-respect, they toss her away like the wrapper on a candy bar. No guy is going to do that to my little sister. Nobody is going to use Basma and then laugh, do you understand, *dude?*"

"What about Mark Huber?" Dustin asked. "Did you ever think that maybe he's trying to use Basma?"

"Never mind about Mark Huber," Nazar said. *"You* just stay away from Basma."

"Dustin, please go," Basma said quietly. "It's better that way."

Dustin looked at Basma and then back at Nazar. He knew he would only make it worse for her if he stayed. He decided that from now on he'd have to make sure he was gone from the gift shop before Nazar arrived. He picked up his sketch pad and pencils and headed for the door.

"Good-bye, Basma," he said. But he got only silence for an answer.

* * *

On Monday morning, Dustin was driving to school when a pair of students on the way to the high school dashed across the street in front of him. He slammed on his brakes in time, but his heart was pounding in his chest. For a split second, the two students looked at him with real terror in their eyes. Then they hurried on across the street.

These near misses happened frequently. In fact, this was the second time this semester that Dustin had narrowly avoided disaster at that same location.

City High was located on Broadway, one of the busiest streets in town. Burgerland, a popular fast-food joint that served breakfast and lunch, was across the street from the school. Kids leaving Burgerland were usually in too much of a hurry to make the long walk to the corner and then circle back to City High. So they dashed directly across the street. Dustin couldn't criticize the students too much. He had done it a few times himself.

"There ought to be a crosswalk and a light here," Dustin muttered to himself. He had written a letter about the problem to the editor of the local paper. He had even written to the city council. They had sent back a nice reply saying that the matter was under study.

But now Dustin was freshly shaken by the close call he'd just had. When he got to journalism class later that morning, he sat right down and sketched a cartoon of a student lying in the middle of Broadway, surrounded by paramedics. Two city officials were standing nearby. One was saying to the other, "Now, let's read the regulations again. How many people have to be injured or killed before we install a light?"

"This is going in the next edition, Joel," Dustin said, handing the editor the cartoon. "The city council is meeting next week. Maybe my cartoon will get people fired up to go to the meeting or call and let the council know how they feel."

Joel raised his bushy eyebrows. "That might be a problem, man," he said. "Mr. Alstead really likes your endangered species cartoon. He showed it to me this morning before school. He says we have to run the cartoon in order for it to make the deadline for that award he wants you to go for."

Just then Mr. Alstead entered the room. Dustin explained the problem. "Mr. Alstead," he said, "I almost hit two students this morning. We've got to light a fire under the city council so they install a crosswalk and light before someone gets killed."

Mr. Alstead looked at the cartoon and shook his head. "Dustin, I understand, and believe me, I applaud your public spirit. But that cartoon doesn't meet the Hogarth award requirements. The topic has to be something kids all over the country can relate to. Your endangered species cartoon is perfect."

"Maybe there are lots of other schools that have traffic problems," Dustin suggested.

"Maybe," Mr. Alstead said. "But you're taking a big chance with it. As I said, the endangered species cartoon is a much more appropriate topic for the contest."

"Couldn't we run both cartoons?" Dustin asked hopefully. "Then I could submit either one."

"Dustin, you know the policy is one cartoon per edition," Mr. Alstead said. "Besides, even if I bent the rules, what would I bump from the paper?"

"How about some of the ads?" Dustin suggested.

"And risk those businesses not advertising again?" Mr. Alstead answered. "We need those sponsors to keep the paper going, Dustin."

"What about an article?" Dustin asked.

"Whose article is it going to be?" Mr. Alstead asked. "Those kids have worked really hard on their submissions. It wouldn't be fair to make them wait another month." Mr. Alstead noticed that Dustin was about to make another suggestion. Before Dustin could speak, the teacher said, "And no, Dustin, we can't add another page. It's too expensive."

"But if the city council doesn't approve the light now," Dustin said, "it'll be another month before they meet again. What if somebody gets hit in the meantime?"

Mr. Alstead leaned forward and placed his hand on Dustin's arm sympathetically. "Dustin," he began, "as I said, it's wonderful that you are so concerned about public safety. But if we run this cartoon, you'll be giving up your chances—and the school's chances—of receiving some very prestigious recognition. We can run the traffic cartoon next month in time for the city council meeting."

"But I'd never forgive myself if some kid got hurt or, worse yet, killed," he said.

"Tell you what," Mr. Alstead said. "I'm going to let you make this call. The deadline for sending the paper to the printer is tomorrow morning at 11:00. Let me know what you decide by then. But as your teacher, I'm recommending that you run the endangered species cartoon. After all, this is your one chance to prove you've got some talent. The Hogarth award could open up a lot of opportunities for you in the future."

At lunch time, Dustin spotted Basma in the usual place. As she looked up, Dustin saw that she looked worried.

"What's the matter, Basma?" he asked.

"Someone stole one of our most expensive figurines last night," she said. "It was worth over 100 dollars."

"What happened?" Dustin asked. "Did you catch who did it?"

Basma shook her head. "We don't know what happened. One minute it was there and the next—poof—it was gone. None of us saw anything."

"That's really too bad, Basma," Dustin

said. Again, Dustin felt sorry for Basma's family. They should not have to suffer at the hands of kids who were probably just out to impress their friends with their daring.

"You look upset too," Basma said. "What's the matter?"

Dustin told her about his dilemma. "You know, I wouldn't be thinking so much about this now," he explained, "but it's such an awful feeling to come that close to hurting someone. For a second this morning, I wasn't sure I'd be able to stop in time."

"Maybe nothing bad will happen, Dustin," Basma suggested. "It has not happened yet."

Dustin shook his head. "It's going to happen sooner or later, Basma. Maybe my cartoon won't make a difference, but if I don't even try, then what am I going to feel like when it happens? My winning the Hogarth might open up opportunities for me, but what good's it going to do for some student who gets killed out there on that street?"

Basma was quiet for a moment. Then she looked straight at Dustin and said, "I think you should run the traffic cartoon, Dustin. I think it is something you have to do."

Dustin struggled with his choices for the rest of the day. That night he had a hard time getting to sleep just thinking about it. He kept seeing the terrified faces of those students who almost ended up on his van.

By morning, Dustin still hadn't made his decision. He looked at his face in the mirror. "Dustin Brand, Caped Crusader," he said aloud in a mock serious voice, "risking his entire future for the good of humankind!" It was almost laughable.

"Hey, man," Dustin's image seemed to say to him. "Don't be more of a bozo than you already are. A couple of airhead students dashed in front of you. You stopped your van, didn't you? Everything worked out fine. That's all there is to it. Nobody appointed you Super Hero of the traffic scene. That's what cops are for. So get real, jerk-face—go with the endangered species cartoon. It might be your best hope for some shred of recognition from your father. Remember, you told yourself you'd do whatever it takes to win that award."

Dustin frowned then, and his reflection frowned back at him. "Okay, man, you've been coasting through life without any real challenges. Now you've got your chance to prove that your spine isn't made of jelly. So what if you don't get that award? Maybe your dad—and a lot of other people—will be proud of you for trying to save someone's life."

Dustin suddenly remembered something his grandfather had once told him. "The important things in life aren't things, Dustin," the older man had said. "They're people."

Dustin thought about that a minute. Suddenly he saw himself in one of his own cartoons. He was standing over two paramedics who were working furiously on an injured student lying in the middle of the street. Dustin was holding the Hogarth award. A reporter with a note pad in his hand and a pencil behind his ear was asking him, "Tell me, Mr. Brand, was it worth it? Would you do it all over again if you had the chance?"

That did it. Caped Crusader or not,
Dustin told his reflection, you're running
that traffic cartoon.

7 On the way to school that morning, Dustin saw several City High students cutting across Broadway from Burgerland. One driver screeched on his brakes when two boys carrying their breakfasts in white paper sacks ran out in front of him. In anger, the driver rolled down his window and yelled, "Use the crosswalk at the corner next time!" Dustin was glad he had made the decision to run the traffic cartoon.

Dustin went to see Mr. Alstead before school started. He wanted to break the news to his teacher early so he wouldn't have to worry about it during geometry. Mrs. Blount was giving a unit test today, and Dustin knew he would need all the concentration he could get.

He found Mr. Alstead in the journalism room gathering things together to take to the printer. "Hi, Mr. Alstead," Dustin said.

"Oh, good morning, Dustin," Mr. Alstead answered. "You look like you've been up all night. Have a hard time making your decision?"

"That's an understatement," Dustin said.

"So, are we running the endangered species cartoon?" Mr. Alstead asked. Dustin could hear the hope in his voice. He hated to disappoint his teacher, but he knew he had to.

"I'm sorry, Mr. Alstead," Dustin said, "but I've got to go with the traffic cartoon."

The teacher sighed, leaned on the edge of his desk, and crossed his arms. "Dustin," he said, "you're absolutely sure you want to do this?"

Dustin nodded. "It's the only way I'm going to be able to live with myself," he said.

"As your teacher," Mr. Alstead warned, "I have to advise against it."

"I know, Mr. Alstead," Dustin said. "But I've put a lot of thought into this. It might not be the smart thing to do in the long run, but it seems like the right thing to do now."

"All right, Dustin," Mr. Alstead said abruptly, returning his attention to his packing. "I'll see you second period." It was obvious to Dustin that the conversation was over.

Dustin had mixed feelings as he left the journalism room. On the one hand, he felt as if a load had been taken off his chest. Right or wrong, the decision had been made, and he no longer had to struggle with it.

On the other hand, though, he felt bad for his teacher. Mr. Alstead had worked hard for over ten years to build up the journalism program at City High. In that time, it had become one of the best in the state. An award like the Hogarth would have reflected well on Mr. Alstead's efforts.

Also Dustin worried that he would regret his decision someday. What if the Hogarth really could have helped him in the future? It would certainly have looked good on college applications. And maybe it would have even increased his chances of getting a scholarship. Then Dustin remembered the reporter in his cartoon asking him, "Was it worth it, Mr. Brand?" Dustin knew that no matter what the Hogarth would have been worth to his future, it was not worth risking another person's life for. He decided that he'd just have to make it as a cartoonist without the award.

Dustin met Basma in the hall on the way to geometry class.

"You look tired," Basma said.

"I am," Dustin answered. "I was up half the night trying to decide which cartoon to run."

"And?" Basma asked.

"I've decided to go with the traffic cartoon," Dustin said.

"Dustin, I am proud of you," Basma said. "You did the right thing. I know you did."

"I sure hope so," Dustin answered.

As they entered the room, Dustin saw Mark Huber in his usual place, waiting for Basma. "You'd better go," he said. "Prince Charming awaits."

"I wish he would leave me alone," Basma said. "I don't understand what he wants with me. He is so wealthy, and my family is struggling just to keep the shop running. What does he want with me?"

"I don't know," Dustin said, "but I'd be careful, Basma. Talk about your hyenas. . ."

Basma smiled. "I'll be careful," she said. "I know how to handle hyenas. Hey, good luck on the test, Dustin. Just remember those things we worked on."

"I will," Dustin answered. "Good luck to you too—as if you're going to need it."

Dustin was nervous as Mrs. Blount passed out the tests. Right now he had a C minus in geometry. To avoid getting a mid-term report, he knew he would have to get at least a C plus on the test.

As Dustin started working, he breathed a sigh of relief. His work with Basma had really paid off. He solved most of the problems on the first try, with only two or three giving him any real difficulty. By the time Dustin was finished, he was elated. He was sure he'd pulled at least a C, if not a B.

Dustin turned in his test and waited for the bell to ring. He could hardly wait to tell Basma after class. But as he left the room, he saw Mark and Basma disappearing down the hall together. Dustin sighed and headed for journalism.

Mr. Alstead was waiting for him. "Dustin," he said, "why don't you go into my office? As soon as I get the class going on their work, I'll be there. I need to talk to you."

Dustin frowned. What could Mr. Alstead want? Was the teacher going to demand that Dustin change his mind about the cartoon? But he couldn't do that. He'd already told Dustin that the choice was up to him. Dustin went to Mr. Alstead's office and waited.

"I think I'm going to have to go back on what I said about leaving the decision up to you," Mr. Alstead said a few minutes later as he entered the office and closed the door.

"What do you mean?" Dustin asked with a sinking feeling in his stomach.

"Do your parents know about this, Dustin?" the teacher asked.

"No," Dustin said. "I don't think they're particularly interested."

"Well, I think it's time they knew," Mr. Alstead said. "I think they should have a say in this too."

"But those cartoons," Dustin protested, "they're mine. I should be able to decide which one runs and which one doesn't."

"Under any other circumstances, I'd agree," Mr. Alstead said. "But too much of your future is at stake here, Dustin. Your parents have a right to know what's at risk."

"Mr. Alstead, my parents don't care," Dustin tried to explain. "All they care about is whether I'm getting good grades or going out for sports. They think cartooning is a waste of time, especially my dad. He wants me to be a computer programmer or something."

"Well, that may be the case, Dustin," Mr. Alstead said. "but your parents don't know that there's a thousand dollars involved here. They have a right to know."

"But, Mr. Alstead, you said the deadline for getting things to the printer was this morning. Isn't it too late to talk to my parents?"

"I just spoke with the printer," Mr. Alstead said. "She says if she lays out the rest of the paper today, she'll still be able to add the cartoon first thing in the morning. She plans on doing a print run tomorrow about 10:00 a.m."

"But Mr. Alstead—" Dustin began.

"I'm sorry I had to go back on my word, Dustin," the teacher said. "But I wouldn't be doing my job if I didn't make your parents aware of this."

Dustin felt sick as he returned to the journalism room. Just when he thought he was finished with this whole business, he'd had the rug pulled out from under him. Why did Mr. Alstead insist on bringing Dustin's parents into this?

8 Dustin was relieved that he had to work at the supermarket that afternoon. At least Dad can't yell at me about the Hogarth until later, he thought.

As Dustin finished bagging a small sack of groceries for an elderly woman, he saw Kimberly and Emma and their boyfriends enter the store. A few minutes later, they entered the checkout lane with a grocery cart full of soda and bottled water. Probably for one of the parties they have every weekend, Dustin thought.

Emma nudged Kimberly when she noticed Dustin. Kimberly smiled smugly. "I can hardly wait until our party," she said loudly.

"Yeah, it's going to be so much fun," Emma said. "Everybody who's anybody will be there."

Dustin bagged the bottles in silence. He knew they were purposely discussing the upcoming party to point out that he wasn't invited. It was their way of getting back at him for the shoplifting incidents.

"Yeah, too bad you can't come, Mr. *Nobody*," Kimberly's boyfriend said to Dustin.

Dustin ignored his comment and placed the last sack into the cart. He started to walk away when he heard Kimberly say, "We need help taking this out to the car."

Oh, great, Dustin thought. He turned around and grabbed the cart amidst snickers from the group.

"We're parked at the far end, grocery boy," Kimberly said as Dustin pushed the cart outside.

"Don't you mean Frankenstein?" Emma's boyfriend asked. "That's what all the kids have called him since seventh grade." They all laughed.

Dustin walked on silently. They came to Kimberly's car, and Dustin began lifting the sacks into the trunk.

"Whoa, look at those bulging muscles," Emma said sarcastically. "You get those from drawing all those cartoons?" Again the group laughed.

"You're pathetic," Dustin said, closing the trunk.

"Pathetic?" Kimberly said. "You're the pathetic one, watching that little foreigner's stupid gift shop. Haven't you got anything better to do?"

Dustin grew angry at hearing the insult aimed at Basma. "You guys are giving our school a bad name. You make everyone think the kids at City High are all a bunch of thieves. Why do you bother stealing? You've got it all, and you want to take it away from people like the Saads who are struggling to make ends meet."

Anger flashed in Kimberly's eyes. She grabbed one of the bottles of cola from the grocery cart, shook it up, and sent a stream of brown liquid at Dustin.

"That'll teach you to accuse me and my friends of shoplifting," Kimberly said. "Come on, guys. Let's get away from this loser."

The four piled into Kimberly's car and roared off, leaving Dustin standing in the parking lot soaking wet. Dustin glanced down at his clothes. A brown stain extended from his chest to his knees. At least I'm almost at the end of my shift, he thought. Then he remembered that his father would probably be waiting to talk to him about his cartoon. Dustin shook his head. This had been a bad day all around.

* * *

Just as Dustin thought, his father was waiting for him when he got home. Dustin could tell by the look on his dad's face that a lecture was coming.

"Dustin," Mr. Brand began, "what's this I hear from Mr. Alstead about some kind of cartoon award?"

"It's the Hogarth award, Dad," Dustin answered. "It's a national contest for high school students."

"Why didn't your mother or I know anything about it?" Dustin's father asked.

"I tried to tell you once, Dad," Dustin said. "You weren't interested."

Mr. Brand shook his head. "I don't remember anything about it," he said. "Nevertheless, your teacher tells me there's a thousand dollars involved here. And that you're thinking of running a different cartoon than the one you originally submitted. Is that right?"

Dustin nodded. Here it comes, he thought.

"Why, Dustin?" his father asked.

Dustin found that he was reluctant to

answer. Other kids' parents asked them questions because they had a genuine interest in their children's affairs. But for some reason, Dustin always felt like his father was putting him on the spot when he asked him questions. Instead of answering, Dustin simply shrugged.

"Dustin, I'm speaking to you," Mr. Brand said. His tone became harder. "Answer me."

"Dad," Dustin began, "why are you taking a sudden interest in my cartooning? You've never cared before."

"We're not talking about pocket change here, son," Mr. Brand said. "We're talking about a thousand dollars. Now why on earth would you jeopardize your chances of winning all that money?"

Dustin sighed. It was obvious he wasn't going to get out of this. He told his father about the traffic cartoon. "It's important to run it, Dad," he said. "It might affect the city council's decision about the cross-walk and light."

"I understand that, Dustin, but the council meets every month. Run the traffic cartoon in the next issue of the paper. Go for the thousand dollars first."

"You just don't get it, do you, Dad? Even if I ran the other cartoon, I wouldn't be doing it to win the money. Sure, the money would be nice, but it's the award itself that's important. The Hogarth could open up a lot of doors for me in the future."

"Well, I wouldn't go so far as to say that," his father said. "I mean, it always looks good to have that kind of thing on your resume. But a cartoon award is not going to get you a job, Dustin."

"It might—as a cartoonist," Dustin said quietly.

"There you go again," Mr. Brand said, shaking his head. "When are you going to face reality, Dustin? When are you going to give up this silly pipe dream about being a famous cartoonist? I've told you and told you that your chances are next to nil."

Suddenly all the frustration and disappointment Dustin had been feeling about his father came to a head. It was bad enough that his father refused to recognize Dustin's cartooning talents. But it was worse that he wouldn't even give Dustin a little credit for trying to save someone's life.

He looked at his father and said slowly and with emphasis, "No, Dad, the question is, when are you going to face reality? I'm never going to be an engineer like Doug or a basketball player like Becky. I'm Dustin. And I want to be a cartoonist. Do you hear me, Dad? A cartoonist!"

Suddenly Dustin could stand it no longer. He fled from the house and jumped into his van. Then he roared down the street, something he rarely did. He wondered if his father found his behavior odd or worrisome. Probably not. He wondered if his father came to the window, rubbing his chin with concern. No, Dustin thought bitterly. Right now his father was probably back at his computer pounding away on the keys. It would have amazed him if someone had told him that he was breaking his son's heart by refusing to acknowledge the only real talent Dustin had.

Dustin drove to a nearby lake, parked, and walked to the water's edge. There he sat down on a rock.

"Dad," he said into the silence, "I hate you. I hate the way you treat me like a worthless fool. I hate how you ignore stuff that is so important to me. I hate how you never talk with me, just at me. You never want to hear what I have to say. You don't think I'm worth listening to. I hate you, I hate you, I hate you." Dustin's eyes filled with tears. Then he thought of his grandfather. Grandpa had listened to Dustin. He'd been excited at every cartoon Dustin had drawn, every little triumph Dustin made. Now Dustin grieved anew at the loss of the white-haired man who could share his life so completely.

Slowly Dustin stood and wiped the tears from his face. He looked up at the cloudless sky. "Hey, Gramps," he said. "I drew this cartoon about the traffic problem at the school. I'm giving up a shot at the Hogarth to save a life or two. Imagine that, huh? Hooray for me. What a hero!"

Dustin's eyes filled with fresh tears as his voice died in the wind. He shook his head and thought, Right. Some hero I am.

Mr. Alstead thinks I'm crazy. My dad thinks I'm crazy. Everyone thinks I'm crazy—everyone except Basma, that is.

Dustin got back into his van and drove to the nearest pay phone.

"Saads' Gift Shop." Dustin was relieved to hear Basma's voice on the other end.

"Basma? Hi, it's me, Dustin."

"Oh, hello, Dustin," Basma said.

"Is your brother around?" Dustin asked.

"Nazar? No, he's at class," Basma answered. "How are you?"

"I guess I've been better," Dustin admitted. He told her about his confrontation with his father. "I've never spoken to him like that before, Basma. But I just had to tell him how I feel."

"It's good that you told him, Dustin," Basma said. "He needs to know how you feel. Then maybe he will accept your dream to be a cartoonist."

"I don't know," Dustin said. "It's hard to say."

"It will get easier with time," Basma said. "You'll see."

Dustin couldn't believe how comforting it was to talk to Basma. At times she seemed wise beyond her years.

"I just hope I did the right thing in running the traffic cartoon," Dustin worried. "What if no one responds to it, and the city council rejects the crosswalk? Then I would have been better off going with the endangered species cartoon. At least I would have had a chance at the Hogarth."

"Dustin, why don't you submit the traffic cartoon anyway?" Basma suggested.

"I don't know," Dustin said. "Mr. Alstead said it didn't meet the requirements, so it's probably no use."

"Do it, Dustin," Basma urged. "The least you can do is lose—and you might win." Basma covered the phone with her hand, and Dustin heard her say, "Just a minute, Mama. I'll be right there."

"I've got to hang up now, Dustin," Basma said. "Will you at least think about submitting the traffic cartoon?"

"Yeah, I'll think about it," Dustin answered. "Hey, thanks for talking to me, Basma. I feel a lot better."

"You're welcome, Dustin," Basma said. "Good-bye."

As Dustin hung up the phone, he thought again about his grandfather. He realized that the older man would agree with Basma that Dustin should enter the traffic cartoon for the Hogarth award. "Go for it, Dusty," he could hear his grandfather saying. "What can it hurt?"

Dustin smiled. What could it hurt? he asked himself. Losing that award certainly couldn't cause him any more grief than his father already had.

9 When Dustin got to school the next morning, he saw that the newspaper racks were filled with the latest edition of the *Sentinel*. He picked one up and looked for the traffic cartoon on the way to geometry class. He was surprised to see that it wasn't in its usual spot on the editorial page. Dustin leafed through the paper and finally located the cartoon on the last page among several advertisements.

"Guess Mr. Alstead's still upset," Dustin said to Basma as he showed her the cartoon in geometry. He was sitting in the desk across from her before class started. "Oh, well," he continued. "At least I tried. Maybe a few kids will see this and go to the city council meeting. I know I'm going to be there."

"Are you going to submit the cartoon for the Hogarth award?" Basma asked.

Dustin shrugged. "I think so. I'm going to get the forms from Mr. Alstead next period."

Just then Mark Huber entered the room and took his seat in front of Basma. Turning around to talk to Basma, he looked at Dustin and said, "Get lost, Brand."

"Sorry, but we were having a conversation before you walked in," Dustin said.

"Well, it just ended," Mark said. "I have something to talk to Basma about."

"Maybe she doesn't want to talk to you," Dustin said.

"Like she'd rather talk to you?" Mark laughed.

"Let's let her decide," Dustin said. "Basma, do you want to talk to me or Mark?"

"Mark, Dustin is right," Basma said. "We were talking about something very important when you came in. Maybe you and I can talk after class."

"Important?" Mark snorted. "What could possibly be important in this dweeb's life? How to draw Mickey Mouse's ears on straight? I've seen the cartoons you do, Brand. If they're meant to be funny, I don't get it."

"They're not *all* meant to be funny," Dustin said. Mark's superior attitude was getting on his nerves. "Some are meant to make a point—but then I don't suppose you'd understand. After all, they *are* written above the first-grade level."

Anger flashed in Mark's eyes, and he started to say something, but just then Mrs. Blount walked in. Dustin knew the bell was about to ring, so he hurried to his seat.

After she had taken attendance, Mrs. Blount opened her briefcase and pulled out a stack of papers. "I have your tests graded, class," she said. "Some of you will be very pleased—and some of you won't. All in all, though, I saw quite a bit of improvement over the last test."

She walked up and down the rows, handing out the papers. Dustin worried. Which group was he in—the one that would be pleased or the one that wouldn't?

"Good job, Dustin," Mrs. Blount said as she handed him his test. "It's amazing what a little effort will do, isn't it?"

Dustin looked at the B at the top of his test. He'd done it! Now he wouldn't get a mid-term. He smiled over at Basma and gave her a thumbs up. She smiled back knowingly.

* * *

"Great cartoon," Joel said to Dustin as Dustin entered the journalism room the next period.

"Yeah, good job, Dustin," another student said. "We've needed that crosswalk for a long time. My friend and I are going to go to the city council meeting. She was almost hit one day last month crossing that street."

"Thanks," Dustin said. "I was hoping my cartoon would have that kind of effect."

Just then Mr. Alstead entered the room. Dustin approached his desk.

"Mr. Alstead," he began, "I think I'd like to submit my traffic cartoon for the Hogarth award."

"I'm afraid you'd just be wasting postage," Mr. Alstead said. "It's a good cartoon, but it's not what they're looking for."

"Probably not," Dustin admitted. "But I'm going to do it anyway. I figure if I don't win this year, I've got two more years to try."

"All right, Dustin," Mr. Alstead said. "Stop into my office after class, and I'll give you the forms."

"Thanks, Mr. Alstead," Dustin said.

That evening Dustin filled out the forms for the award. He put them, along with the required six copies of the printed cartoon, into an envelope addressed to the Hogarth Award Selection Committee.

He was just getting ready to seal the envelope when he heard a knock on his door.

"Dustin?" he father said, opening the door a crack. "Can I come in?"

"Sure, Dad," Dustin said.

"What are you doing?" Mr. Brand asked, sitting down on the bed.

"Just getting my cartoon ready to submit for the Hogarth award."

"The traffic cartoon? But I thought Mr. Alstead said it didn't meet the requirements," his father said.

"It probably doesn't," Dustin said. "But I'm going to submit it anyway."

"What made you decide to do this?" Mr. Brand asked.

"My friend Basma said I should," Dustin answered as he sealed the envelope. He turned and looked at his father. "I suppose you think it's foolish."

"No, actually I admire you for doing this," Mr. Brand admitted. "Look, Dustin, I know I haven't been the most understanding father when it comes to your dreams. It must seem like I'm always there for Doug and Becky and never there for you."

Dustin shrugged. "Sometimes it feels like that," he said.

Mr. Brand sighed. "I don't know what's the matter with me," he said. "I just want the best for my kids so bad that sometimes I forget what *they* want. The idea of your being a cartoonist seemed so far-fetched to me. I felt like it was my duty to steer you to a more practical career, my being a counselor and all. But I've decided that I was wrong. And I just want you to know that I'm here for you from now on. Whatever help I can give you, I will."

"You were wrong?" Dustin asked. He'd never heard his father say that before.

"Yes. After seeing how you've stood up for your beliefs over this cartoon issue, I realized something about you that I hadn't realized before. If you really want something bad enough, you'll get it."

Dustin looked down at his hands. "I

really do want to be a cartoonist, Dad," he said.

Mr. Brand smiled and said, "I know you do, son. And I'm behind you all the way!"

10 At school the next day, Dustin looked forward to seeing Basma. He wanted to tell her that his cartoon was officially entered. He also wanted to invite her to go to the city council meeting with him the following Tuesday. He thought maybe he had a chance since he didn't think her mother could construe a public meeting as a date. But when he arrived at class, Mark Huber was monopolizing Basma's time, as usual.

Dustin had to wait until lunch time to talk to Basma.

"I'm kind of excited about the city council meeting next Tuesday," he told her. "Several kids have told me that they're going to attend. Do you think your family would let you go with me? It's just a meeting, you know. It's not like it's a real date or anything."

"Oh, Dustin, I was hoping you would ask," said Basma. "But I don't know if they will let me."

Suddenly Dustin had an idea. "I know," he said. "Tell them that you're learning about government for civics class. It would be the truth because you really will learn a lot."

"Good idea," Basma said. "I'll tell them it's an educational experience and that you're just giving me a ride there. Then I think they will let me go."

"Great," Dustin said. "I'll pick you up at the shop around 6:30. The meeting starts at 7:00."

By the end of the school day, Dustin was walking on air. That afternoon, a few more students and two teachers had told him they were going to the meeting. For the first time, he was optimistic that the city council might actually approve the crosswalk.

Dustin was also looking forward to taking Basma to the meeting. It would be the first time spent with her outside of school and the gift shop. He had told her it wasn't a real date, but deep down inside he felt like it was.

* * *

At 6:30 sharp the next Tuesday, Dustin pulled up to the gift shop. He was still in a good mood and could hardly wait for the evening to begin. Basma was just coming out of the back room as he entered the shop. Dustin glanced around—no Nazar, which made it even better.

"Ready to go?" Dustin asked, smiling.

"Yes," Basma said. "Oh, wait. I forgot my purse. I'll be right back."

While Dustin waited for Basma, he heard someone enter the store. Dustin peeked around the end of the display case he was standing next to. His good mood suddenly dissipated. Mark Huber had entered the shop. Dustin wondered what Mark wanted and was just about to say something when he realized that Mark had not seen him. Mark glanced quickly around the store and headed up the far aisle.

Very quietly Dustin moved to where he could see Mark. He was standing by a display of figurines. As Dustin watched, Mark took two figurines off the shelf and put one in each pocket of his jacket. Then he glanced around again, saw that no one was looking, and headed up the aisle toward the front counter. Dustin stayed where he was, watching.

Just then Basma and Nazar came out of

the storeroom. Basma had her purse over her shoulder. "I still don't think you should go, no matter what our mother says," Nazar was saying. "That boy may still be a hyena. One never knows."

"Hi, guys," Dustin heard Mark say. "What's going on?"

"Oh, hello, Mark," Basma said. She sounded surprised. "I didn't know you were here. Where's Dustin?"

Just then Dustin stepped forward. "Here I am, Basma," he said. Nazar glared at him.

"Are you ready to go?" Basma asked, coming out from behind the counter. Obviously she was anxious to leave.

"In a minute," Dustin said. "I think Mark has something to show us first."

Mark looked puzzled. "What do you mean? I just stopped in to say hi to Basma." He looked at Basma. "I was going to ask you to a movie, but I can see you have other plans with Mr. Loony Toons here. So I'll be seeing you." Quickly he turned to go.

"Hold on," Dustin said, placing his hand firmly on Mark's arm. "You haven't shown us what's in your pockets, Mark."

"What is going on?" Nazar demanded.

"You talk about hyenas," Dustin said. "There's your hyena, and he's got the goods to prove it. I saw him pocket two of your figurines while you were in the back room."

Basma gasped.

"What are you talking about?" Nazar asked. "Mark is rich. Why would he steal?"

"I'm not sure," Dustin said. "Let's ask Mark. Why don't you take those things out of your pockets, Mark, and then tell us why you took them?"

Mark sighed loudly and rolled his eyes. He looked as if he were bored with the whole situation. Reluctantly, he removed the figurines from his pocket and placed them on the counter.

"Mark!" Basma said. "Why would you steal from us? I thought you liked us."

Mark shook his head and laughed. "I was just pretending to like you," he said.

"But why?" Basma asked.

Mark shrugged. "It made it easier to steal from you. Every time I came into this place, I nabbed something."

"What else have you taken?" Basma asked.

"Oh, a paperweight, a couple of necklaces—I forget what else," Mark said.

Nazar was standing behind the counter glaring at Mark. Now he placed his hand on the telephone. "You *are* a hyena!" he sneered at Mark. "I'm calling the police."

"Wait, Nazar," Dustin said. "Mark, you still haven't told us why you were shoplifting."

"For kicks, man," Mark said. "Plain and simple."

"But you've got everything a kid could want," Dustin said. "A new car, a fancy house. What do you want with a few figurines from a gift shop?"

Mark looked at Dustin like he was most naive person in the world. "That's just it," he said. "My parents buy me everything. They take me on trips. Do you know I've been to Disney World four times? They do everything for me. There's only so much of that you can take, man, before you get bored. So I steal—just for the thrill of it."

Now Dustin knew why Mark acted as he did. He'd never been taught any differently.

"Would you be willing to return all the merchandise if we don't call the police?" Dustin asked.

"I don't care if you call the police," he said. "My parents will get me out of it."

"Think about it, Mark," Dustin said. "You don't want shoplifting on your record if you can avoid it. No one will ever trust you again."

"Why would you do that for me?" Mark wanted to know. "You've never liked me."

"No, you've never really liked *me*—or anybody, for that matter," Dustin said. "Maybe if Nazar lets you go this time, that'll change, huh?" Dustin turned to Nazar. "Would you be willing to let him go if he returns the stuff he stole?"

Nazar thought for a moment. "If he returns the merchandise—and works for me three nights a week for one month," he said coldly. "Starting today."

"What would I do?" Mark asked.

"Stock shelves," Nazar said. "And look for shoplifters. You should be good at it."

Mark shrugged. "Sure, I guess I could give that a try."

Dustin smiled. "Then it's a deal, Nazar?"

he asked.

Nazar looked at Dustin closely. "It's a deal," he said. Then he smiled. "Now get going, or you will be late for your meeting, *Dustin.*"

Dustin smiled as he and Basma headed out the door. That Nazar wasn't too bad a guy after all, he thought.

When Dustin and Basma got to the meeting, the room was filled with teachers and students from City High. Many of the students had brought their parents with them as well.

"Wow, what a crowd," Dustin said. "I never expected this." He and Basma took the last two seats at the back of the room.

When the council members got to traffic issues, several students and parents rose from their seats and gave testimony in support of the crosswalk. Even Dustin stood up and told about the close calls he had experienced with students cutting across Broadway. After a little more discussion, the issue was put to a vote. The members voted unanimously to allocate funds to install a light and crosswalk.

After the meeting, Dustin was

approached by a man with a camera and notepad. "I'm Raul Gonzales, a reporter from *The City News*," he said. "Someone told me you drew this cartoon that ran in your school newspaper." He held up a copy of Dustin's cartoon.

Dustin nodded. "Yes, I did," he said.

"Well, I'm going to be writing an article on tonight's meeting for tomorrow's paper," Mr. Gonzales said. "And I was wondering if you'd allow me to run your cartoon with the article. I think it was your cartoon that caused this kind of turnout tonight."

Dustin was surprised. "Well, sure, I guess so," Dustin said.

"Great," said the reporter. He asked Dustin for his name, age, and address. "You'll see it in the morning edition."

"Did you hear that, Basma?" Dustin asked. "The paper's going run my cartoon. Isn't that great?"

"Oh, Dustin, I'm so happy for you," Basma said. "Now your father cannot help but be impressed."

"Yeah," Dustin agreed, smiling. "That's for sure."

Dustin left the meeting feeling as if he had actually used his talents to accomplish something good. More than ever, he knew he had made the right decision.

* * *

Two weeks later, Mr. Alstead approached Dustin on the way to geometry class. "Dustin, I need to talk to you," he said. "I heard from the Hogarth award committee. I'm sorry to have to tell you this, but you didn't win the award. As I thought, your cartoon just didn't fit the criteria."

Dustin shrugged. "That's okay, Mr. Alstead. I didn't really think I'd win." He started to walk away.

"Hold on," the teacher said. "I do have some good news for you, too. Evidently, the committee was very impressed by your work. They sent me information on other contests that would accept your traffic cartoon. Some of them are worth a lot of money. One even offers a scholarship to the college of your choice. Are you interested?"

"You bet I am!" Dustin said.

"There's probably quite a bit of paperwork," Mr. Alstead warned. "You might need some help filling it all out."

"That's all right," Dustin said as they headed toward the teacher's office. He thought about what his dad had said about giving him all the help he needed. "Bring on the forms. I know just the person to help me!"

* * *

The next weekend, Dustin and Basma headed to the desert. They packed food and soda, and Basma brought along her camera.

"See how the city sort of drops off out here?" Dustin pointed out. "Now we're in the hills. Pretty soon we'll go through the mountains and then end up in the desert on the other side."

"It's beautiful out here away from the city," Basma said.

"I know," Dustin said. "When my grandfather was alive, he used to take me out here. He loved the desert. He had this old dune buggy he'd haul behind his truck, and we'd ride all over in it. It was great."

"What else did you and your grandfather do?" Basma asked.

"Lots of things," Dustin said. "We used to go fishing together a lot. And once he took me to an exhibit of famous political cartoons at the art center. He knew how interested I was in cartooning. He's the one who really encouraged me to keep drawing them, you know. He had faith that I'd be a great cartoonist someday."

"You must have loved your grandfather a lot," Basma said.

"How can you tell?" Dustin asked.

"Oh, I could see it in your eyes just now," Basma answered. "And the way you smile when you talk about him. It's obvious your memories of him are very warm and full of love."

"Yeah," Dustin said. "He was only in his sixties when he died. When he was in the hospital, I'd visit him almost every day. Sometimes I'd help him eat because he got kind of shaky toward the end. But sometimes I'd just sit and read to him. He loved that. Grandpa knew he was dying, and so did I. Sometimes it would really get me down, and I'd cry. But he always did things to cheer me up. One day he told me that dying is like when you stand on the shore and watch a ship disappear beyond the horizon. You're sad to see the ship get smaller and smaller. But somewhere, on the other side, that ship is getting bigger and bigger. And there's another shore and a happy landing there."

Basma reached over and caressed Dustin's cheek. "That's nice," she said.

Dustin glanced at her lovely face and then returned his eyes to the road. He was sure that suddenly the sights along the highway had grown more beautiful. The orange poppies appeared more brilliant, and the lupine covering the hills was a more radiant blue.

"You know, your grandfather was right," Basma said as they entered the mountains.

"About what?" Dustin asked.

"About your becoming a great cartoonist," Basma answered.

"You think so?" Dustin asked.

"I know so, *dude,*" Basma answered.

Dustin laughed and covered her hand with his. This was going to be a great trip.

Novels by Anne Schraff

PASSAGES

An Alien Spring
Bridge to the Moon
   (Sequel to *Maitland's Kid*)
The Darkest Secret
Don't Blame the Children
The Ghost Boy
The Haunting of Hawthorne
Maitland's Kid
Please Don't Ask Me to Love You
The Power of the Rose
   (Sequel to *The Haunting of Hawthorne*)
The Shadow Man
The Shining Mark
   (Sequel to *When a Hero Dies*)
To Slay the Dragon
   (Sequel to *Don't Blame the Children*)
A Song to Sing
Sparrow's Treasure
Summer of Shame
   (Sequel to *An Alien Spring*)
The Vandal
When a Hero Dies

PASSAGES 2000

Just Another Name for Lonely
   (Sequel to *Please Don't Ask Me to Love You*)
Memories Are Forever
The Hyena Laughs at Night
Gingerbread Heart
The Boy from Planet Nowhere